Hello. My name is Patricia Casey.

This building is Wood Green Animal Shelter. It's a place in the city where sick, stray or abandoned animals are looked after. It's always busy. Happy, sad and funny things happen every minute. After visiting a few times, I decided to bring my camera and pencils along. I had a plan – to make you this book!

For Les Rollings

who told me, "It's the way you touch an animal
for the first time that will gain its confidence"

And for all the staff at
Wood Green Animal Shelter

thank you for opening your door so many times to share
your experiences with me

A percentage of the royalties
from this book is being donated to
Wood Green Animal Shelters,
Registered Charity No. 298348.

The publisher and artist are grateful to
Wood Green Animal Shelters for permission
to make reference to Wood Green Animal Shelter
in the title and content of this book.

First published 2001 by Walker Books Ltd
87 Vauxhall Walk, London SE11 5HJ

10 9 8 7 6 5 4 3 2 1

This book has been typeset in Futura Bold
and Providence Sans

Printed in Hong Kong

British Library Cataloguing in Publication Data:
a catalogue record for this book is available
from the British Library

ISBN 0-7445-6178-7

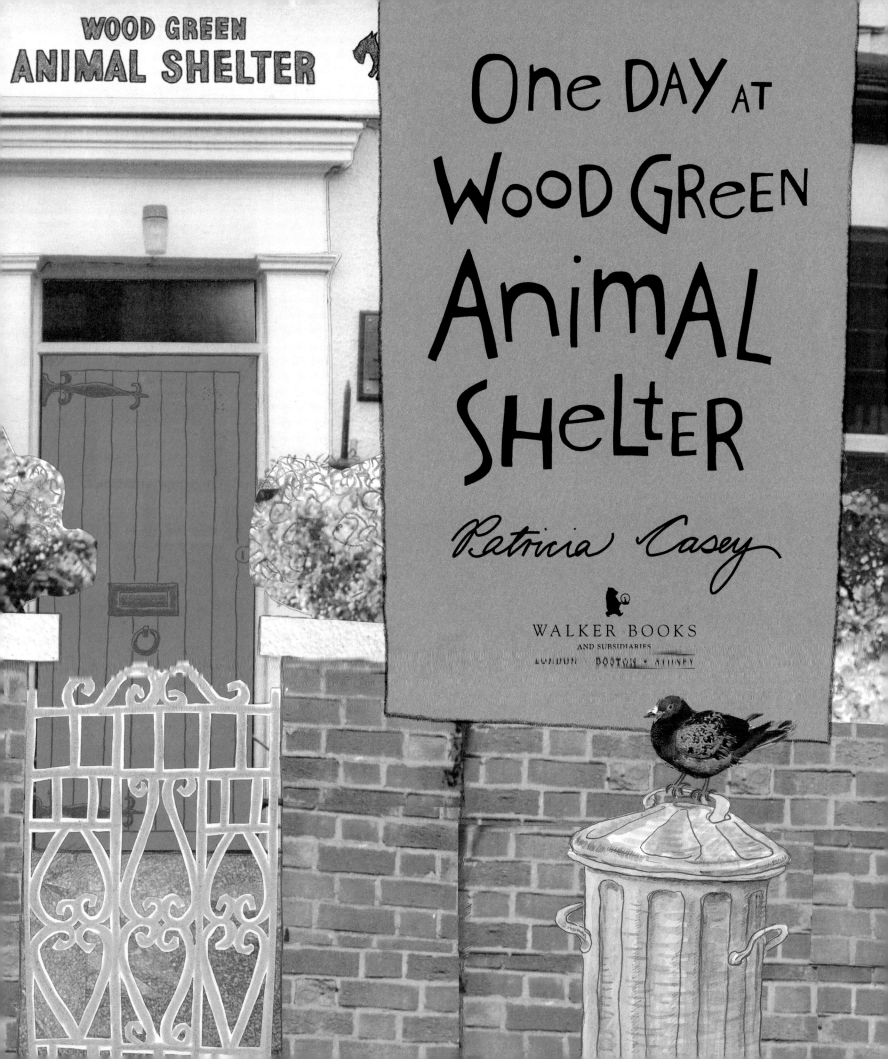

WOOD GREEN
ANIMAL SHELTER

ONE DAY AT WOOD GREEN ANIMAL SHELTER

Patricia Casey

WALKER BOOKS
AND SUBSIDIARIES
LONDON · BOSTON · SYDNEY

The shelter opens at a quarter to eight.
Here comes everyone for work.

Les, the manager, has the keys.
(That's Tandy, his Alsatian dog, on the lead.)
Kelly is carrying a box. (I wonder what's inside?)
Wendy is carrying William, a fox she looks after.
Debbie, the nurse, has brought Gladstone, her bulldog.

And I am here too, with my camera.
Tuppence, the shelter cat, is very pleased to see us.
That's her on the doorstep.

"Swee!" cheeps Kelly's box as we go inside. Tandy pads upstairs to Les's office.

8

Now Angela, Colin, Neil, Rikky and Alison arrive. Altogether, nine people work at the shelter.

Angela gets the waiting-room and surgery ready for the day.

Wendy and William go to the downstairs office.

Debbie takes Gladstone to the back room. Kelly and her cheeping box go too. Alison checks Topsy and Timmy, two stray kittens who stayed overnight.

In the washroom, Colin and Rikky get food ready for the cats who live in the cat sanctuary outside.

Can you hear the cats? Let's go and see what they are doing.

Look! They're s t r e t c h i n g and ya w n ing, and scratching and washing. They're uncurling and stepping out of their little houses. They're pacing and waiting and thinking about ...

breakfast!

Back inside I see what's in Kelly's box. "He's a baby pigeon," Kelly tells me. "He fell out of his nest onto the street. I call him Roast Potato – because he's small enough to fit in my hand, like a potato!"

Roast Potato has a big song for such a small bird!

Until Roast Potato is old enough to look after himself, Kelly will care for him night and day. Roast Potato is too young to fly, but he likes going for walks.

Swee, swee!

He has a little drink with Timmy, the kitten. (They don't know cats and birds don't get on.)

Swee, swee!

He goes for a walk on his breakfast pigeon-mix.

Sweeeeeee!

He goes for a walk up Gladstone's back.

It's true!

Gladstone looks fierce, but he's a softy. He came to the shelter when he was a pup. His owners had been cruel to him.

Debbie took one look at him, and that was it – **LOVE!** She adopted him. They go everywhere together.

Gladstone's tail is so short that when he's happy he wags his whole bottom.

His skin looks too big for him. He is all crinkles and wrinkles and creases and folds.

·ROSIE· ·TOOTS· ·FLUFF· SNAZZLE ·SP

Cat
Quench

The smoothest bit of Gladstone
is his lovely pink
tongue. It is always
out instead of in!
Gladstone gives
the kittens' tummies a good lick –
just as if he was their mummy. Then
he gives Roast Potato's tummy such
a good lick, Roast Potato falls over.

It's
true!

William, the fox, came to the shelter with his sister, Anna, when they were only three days old.

"They were unearthed from their burrow under a building site," says Wendy. "Anna was a healthy cub. But William was sick. First he had colic, then pneumonia, and next he went bald!"

While we talk, William lets me stroke him. Now his fur is thick and silky-soft. His eyes are red-gold. They can see in the dark.

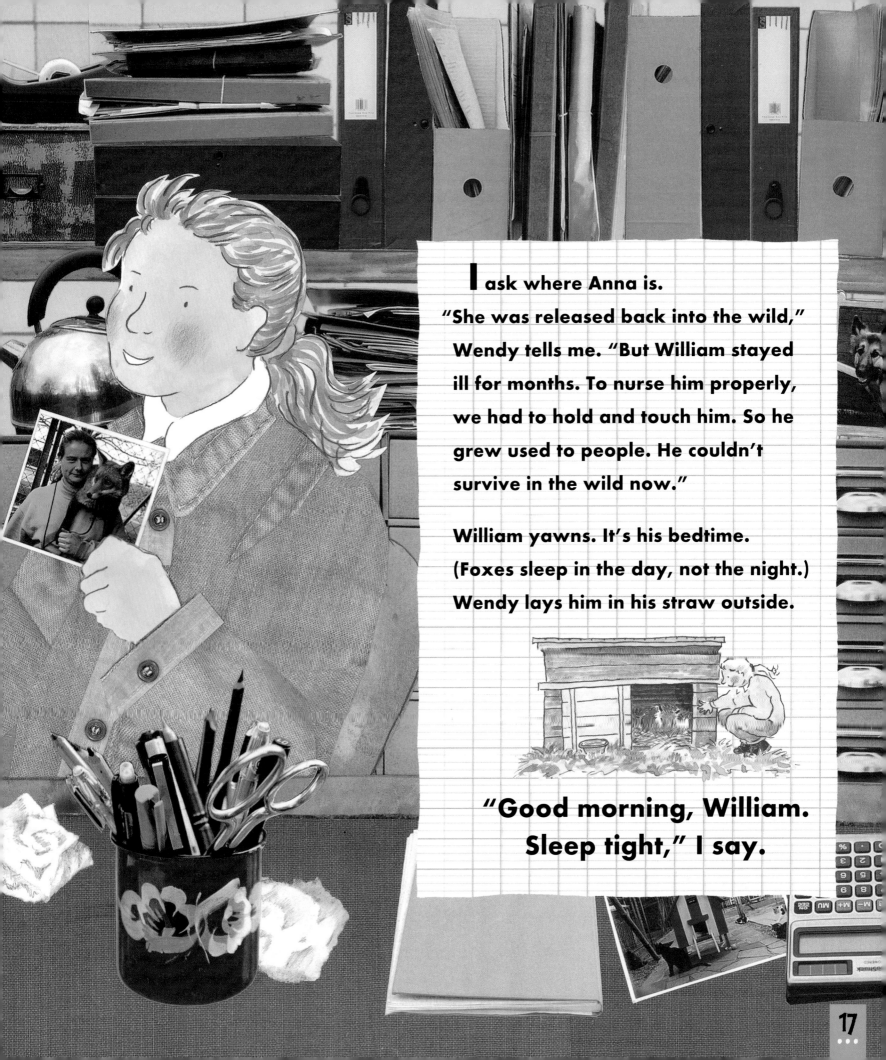

I ask where Anna is.
"She was released back into the wild,"
Wendy tells me. "But William stayed
ill for months. To nurse him properly,
we had to hold and touch him. So he
grew used to people. He couldn't
survive in the wild now."

William yawns. It's his bedtime.
(Foxes sleep in the day, not the night.)
Wendy lays him in his straw outside.

**"Good morning, William.
Sleep tight," I say.**

LIQUID PARAFFIN

SURGICAL SPIRIT

DOG TONIC

tweezers

scissors

cotton-wool

useful bowl

Mr Simmonds listens to Rolley's heart through his stethoscope. Boom, boom, boom. "That sounds in good tick, Rolley," he says.

bandage

clippers

Shampoo
Wet coat and
leave for 2 mins
Rinse
Repeat weekly

Ear
Drops

thermometers

SKIN
SCRUB

FLEA
AWAY
POWDER

Vijay knows that Rolley is never scared with Mr Simmonds.
Debbie fetches more heart pills. "One a day, with food," she says.

I go upstairs to visit Les, the manager, and Tandy. "Someone just rang to say she saw a young deer in the cemetery," Les says. "It needs to be with other deer. Will you and Neil go and rescue it in the ambulance?"

Zoom Broom!

Neil and I find the deer asleep behind a gravestone!

SHELTER FROM THE STORM

We are just about to catch it with our blanket when …

HUP!

It leads Neil on a real wild-deer chase!

IN LOVING MEMORY

NEAR AND YET SO FAR

MISSING YOU

GONE BUT NOT FORGOTTEN

JOURNEY'S END

Don't be frightened, deery.

We drive the little frightened deer to a wood where Neil knows other deer live.
I open the back door and …

HUP!

ANIMAL AMBULANCE

Back at the shelter, lots of new animals have arrived.

Angela is feeding a baby hedgehog with warm goat's milk. "A little boy found it in his garden. It was all alone without a mother," she tells us.

She shows me a dazed song thrush. "It bumped into a lady's greenhouse," she tells me. "Soon it will be well enough to fly away."

Rikky is dusting a cat with flea powder. "She's a 'doorstep cat'," he says. "Someone didn't want her, so they rang the bell and ran away. It happens often."

Debbie and Kelly are bandaging splints round a pigeon's broken leg. "Pigeons' legs are so small," says Debbie, "we are using lollipop sticks. It should be healed in two weeks."

Alison tells me about a little girl who brought a gecko in. "It climbed into her mum's suitcase when they were in Spain," she says. "They only found it when they unpacked. It's come a long way. They don't know how to look after it, so we will."

"Another little girl tried to bring her lame pony right into the surgery!" Les tells me. "I told them to wait outside. This is not a stable!"

The day is nearly over. Colin's made some coffee. What a busy day it's been! Everyone deserves a cup.

William has woken up.
He likes coffee for his breakfast too.
Mmmm! Coffee fingers.

William may be wide-awake, but the other animals are tired. Sleep well, Timmy and Topsy.

Goodnight, Doorstep Cat. Goodnight, Gecko. Goodnight, Lollipop Pigeon.

The baby hedgehog will need feeding through the night. Angela makes a nest to carry it home in.

The cats in the cat sanctuary are curling up.

Roast Potato and Gladstone are waiting to go home. So is Tandy.

Tuppence will see everyone again tomorrow.

Goodnight, everyone.
Goodnight,
Wood Green Animal Shelter,
until another day.

Index

ambulance  22–23

 bandaging ... 25

cat sanctuary ... 9–11, 27

check-up ... 19–21

 flea powder ... 24

food ... 9, 11, 13, 24, 27

love ... 14

sleep ... 17, 27

stethoscope ... 20

 stray ... 3, 9, 19

the wild ... 17

vet ... 18–21

Look up the pages to find out about all these animal-shelter things.

About the Artist

Patricia Casey has written and illustrated several books for children — but this is the first time she used a camera and a tape-recorder to help her.